About the Author

Pat lives in the North West of England with her husband David. This is her first short story which she says was inspired from an early age by her love and respect of animals. Encouraged not just by her mother or from reading books such as Black Beauty, but also by the attachments she formed with the many strays she brought home as a young child. Pleading to keep them and make them better. Having lived periodically in Spain she was always deeply affected by the plight of abandoned and ill treatment of animals. And hopes this book, in parts, reflects that.

C for Cat (Ceefor)

NIGHTINGALE PAPERBACK

A CIP catalogue record for this title is
available from the British Library.
ISBN 9781838750404

Nightingale Books is an imprint of
Pegasus Elliot MacKenzie Publishers Ltd.
www.pegasuspublishers.com

First Published in 2021

Nightingale Books
Sheraton House Castle Park
Cambridge England

Printed & Bound in Great Britain

Pat Jones

C for Cat (Ceefor)

Nightingale Books

Dedication

To Karl, Maisie and my mum. Forever my teachers of stoicism, love and kindness, and loved beyond measure. Fly butterflies fly.

PART ONE
Winter

On a dark windswept night, as the rain poured down heavily on a Spanish hillside, a small thin shadow slowly edged his way up the steep hill towards a cluster of houses. In the darkness, the glow of the street lights silhouetted the white houses eerily beneath the backdrop of the mountain, throwing long grey shadows into the night.

The figure moved forward cautiously, frequently stopping. Listening, alert and watchful yet little realising that this night too, he was being watched.

Ceefor, a feral cat, was homeless and hungry. Foraging daily for scraps of food, forever searching for shelter, he was weary. But tonight, it was more than hunger that pushed him slowly up the hillside. He was in trouble, wracked with pain.

It was late December in the Jalon Valley, a small village in the mountains of eastern Spain, and even though the temperatures were warm at this time of year, the evenings could be incredibly cold, with long sporadic bouts of torrential rain.

In the summer, this was a lush valley of orange groves, almond trees and vineyards, but at times, in winter, the rain that sometimes lasted for days, gushed down the stony mountainside, filling the old dry river bed and covering the old stone bridge that connected the village to the houses on the hillside.

When this happened, Ceefor knew where to head for. He had made the journey many times over the years. The corner house, where scraps of food mysteriously appeared whenever he showed up, had been his refuge on many occasions, but tonight was different. The chronic cough which had manifested itself over many months had weakened him and the usual spring in his steps was missing. Ceefor had lived with this cough for some time, as did many of the feral cats living rough in rural parts of Spain, but this was not the cause of his suffering. It was the throbbing pain in his back leg which was making him miserable and making his walking laboured and tiresome. It wasn't that Ceefor was an old cat – he wasn't – but at times like this, he was getting tired of sleeping in cold wet places near rubbish bins, or being on his guard constantly for other feral cats in the campo.

His problems had begun over two weeks ago now, ever since he'd jumped a high-gated wall escaping from two barking dogs, and had landed with a heart-quickening thud on the concrete top. The tramps of the road, as the two dogs were named locally, were new to the area, mysteriously appearing from nowhere one day and happily settling in the valley.

One was a short-haired bitch that looked like a cross between a retriever and a German hunting dog. Probably that's what she was, once upon a time, until the farmer decided she didn't hunt for rabbits quickly enough anymore, and simply turned her out. The other animals in the valley, Rock Rat, Ginge and a Spanish podenco dog, named her Blanco because of her colour. She looked to be a young dog, but her appearance indicated that she had been a tramp of the road for some time. No one knew her story. No one, that was, except Blanco. Her coarse white hair was dirty and dull from years of neglect and, on her legs, she had weeping sores beneath areas of matted coat.

Tagging alongside her was a smaller dog, similar in size to a Jack Russell. This little one had been named Nero and he was totally different: short, stocky, with strong muscles and in much better health. Nero made himself the leader and everywhere that Nero went, Blanco would follow nonchalantly behind him, always walking as a pair, as though they had a purpose, an urgent need to be somewhere. Of course, the need was usually to search for food and shelter, or perhaps just a need for a bit of human kindness.

It wasn't that Ceefor was afraid of the tramps of the road, he wasn't; but his failing health had slowed him down considerably and he knew that if they chased him again, he simply didn't have the strength, energy or fitness to outrun them.

As Ceefor continued slowly up the hill, every so often he would stop and listen. Sounds and movements in the long grasses along the verge unnerved him. He hated living with this agonizing pain, but even more he hated the fatigue which gripped him, forcing him to limp. Still, in spite of that, he was determined to keep going. As he approached the villa, he became more nervous, keeping his tail next to his body and once more stopping many times to listen. A noise in the undergrowth halted his steps, so he stopped and waited. Many of the feral cats hunted at night near

the houses, and wild boar frequently came down from the mountain, digging around the trees for truffles. If disturbed, the wild boar could be dangerous, so Ceefor always kept well clear of their tracks. He wondered whether the noise might be Ginge, the toothless cat that lived in the campo near the green Nissen hut.

Ginge was a very old cat. Over the years she had lost most of her teeth and had difficulty eating, but she had found a small hole in the side of the Nissen hut and squeezed herself in, rarely leaving her hiding place unless she was really starving. Then she would squeeze out in the hope that people passing by might feed her. She wasn't always old though; once upon a time, when she was young and lived as a kitten with a local family, everyone made a fuss of her. They would stroke and cuddle her and talk to her for hours. So, in a way, she did know what kindness was, but when the people moved away, they simply left her behind. After a while of fending for herself, her body got thinner, her fur became patchy and she grew older. People didn't want to know her then and would shoo her away from their houses. Over time, her health had deteriorated, her looks had changed and, with her missing teeth and dirtiness, people seemed to judge her on what they saw and didn't want to talk to her or touch her. Everyone loved kittens and, inside her head, Ginge was still a playful kitten, still the same cat she had always been. The sad thing was that no one could see that; they just saw her appearance. Now her life had been carved out differently and no one much cared about her these days, which was sad in many ways.

Ceefor approached the house and entered the back way, under cover of the bushes close to the garage. A few lights were on in the house as he made his way to the side entrance where the window to the kitchen was usually open – it was closed. Big metal shutters were on the windows and patio door and once past the door, he headed to the pool house. Outside the pool house door, the scraps were there and greedily Ceefor ate them as quickly as he could, unaware of a face at the window.

Quitely, the kitchen door opened and ever so quietly little footsteps tip-toed across the patio. The little girl with long brown hair, blue eyes and a slender body inched her way slowly towards the pool house, trying to be very quiet whilst gingerly stepping over puddles in her bare feet. This was Lucy, or Lucy Lou, as her friends liked to call her. Lucy was ten and had no brothers or sisters. She was slim for her age, not as tall as the other girls in her class, as they liked to remind her, but Lucy had something they didn't; Lucy had a secret.

Lucy loved Ceefor, even though Ceefor didn't know that. He didn't know what the word love meant and he certainly didn't know that Lucy waited every night when it rained, hoping for him to visit her. Looking out of her bedroom window down the road, she always waited. Her parents didn't know this either, which is why it was a secret. They thought she was in bed, fast asleep, but Lucy knew that whenever it rained very hard, Ceefor couldn't get over the bridge and he would come to where he knew he could get food.

As Lucy neared the pool house, she gently and quietly called his name, Ceefor. But Ceefor didn't know he had a name, his name. No one except Lucy had ever tried to speak to him and it was only Lucy that had given that name, C for cat. She whispered it again, a little louder, so he could hear.

The sound of a human voice unnerved Ceefor and, as quickly as he had eaten, he bolted off straight into the bushes and sat, watching. Lucy followed in his direction and crouched close to the bush, again speaking quietly as she repeated, "Hello, Ceefor."

Ceefor edged further into the bushes, his hissing sound warning her not to come closer. Although he was not afraid of Lucy, he was terribly nervous. He had seen this little girl many times and she had always held her hand out with food in it, but it was only when she dropped the food on the floor that he dared to grab it and run.

Tonight, though, his swift movements into the bushes had increased his leg pain and, as he retreated, he yelped. The sound of Ceefor's cry alarmed Lucy. Her instincts immediately told her that Ceefor was in trouble and he needed help. But how could she help him, she wondered. Lucy had always been a thoughtful, considerate child, sympathetic not just to animals, but to her friends in school as well. And

for as long as she could remember, she had always wanted a pet, but her parents had totally dismissed the idea because they travelled a lot. Their house in Spain was a holiday home that they all came to in the winter months, so it would have been difficult to keep an animal. Lucy didn't want to understand this, she so desperately wanted a pet, but over time she respected her parents' decision, even though sometimes she didn't like it.

Lucy only saw Ceefor in the winter months, so she had no idea where he went to in the summer, but ever since she had first seen him as a kitten by the bins, noticing his white-tipped tail, she had longed to own him. Then, as he grew and she grew, she watched from a distance, seeing his getting older and how his fur changed from soft silky fur to the thick stiff fur he now had. One Christmas, when she was about eight years old, her parents asked her what she wanted for Christmas. It would have been her dearest wish to have a pet, but she knew from the many times of asking what the answer would be. Instead, she made a second choice, a pair of binoculars. These she took to Spain and, whenever the heavy rains came, she kept them by her bed and kept a close eye on the road leading up from the village to the houses. Even though Ceefor was a small cat, she would always see him making his way to her house. The darkness hid his brown and tan shape, but Lucy had her binoculars focused on his white-tipped tail and four white paws, and she knew the route he took.

Now faced with this dilemma, Lucy pondered

what to do and how she was going to help Ceefor. At ten years old, she had no knowledge of what could be wrong with him, but she did know the sound of a painful cry and knew she had to do something. Thinking quickly, she returned to the house. It was late and her parents were still deep in conversation with their friends, so she knew she would have a bit of time. But a bit of time to do what? She could be in more trouble by keeping this secret to herself. Then she thought about what her mum did for her when she was sick.

She looked for the keys to the pool house. Then she went back to her bedroom and picked up a small cushion, tucking it under her arm. Quietly, she went into the small room off the kitchen where she knew her mum had a hot water bottle. Her mum always filled that for her when she had a tummy ache, so maybe that would be the right thing for Ceefor.

Hurriedly, she took them out to the pool house, opened the door and slid them onto the floor. Again, she went back into the house and this time she found an old saucer and some milk, and managed to reach the cupboard where she knew a bottle of medicine her mum kept for her, for when she had a sore throat, was kept. Taking it down from the cupboard, she stuck it in her pocket and, with the other hand free, she picked up a spoon.

Now she felt better; she could go and do something.

Equipped, she headed out into the rainy night

and once inside the pool house, she carefully mixed a teaspoon of the medicine with the milk in the saucer, stirring it thoroughly. She placed the cushion on the floor next to it and then she put the semi-warm hot water bottle to the side of the cushion.

She thought carefully about the next thing to do. Although she had a good place for Ceefor, she also realised that at this particular time, Ceefor didn't know what was best for him. Having no identifiable language between them was difficult. If only she could convey to him how much she wanted to help him, but then she thought perhaps just kindness was the identifiable language. If everyone was kind to each other, she reasoned with herself, there would be no need for different languages.

Lucy now had to entice Ceefor into the pool house. He was still hiding in the bushes. Again she thought hard until another plan took shape in her mind. She remembered her mum sprinkling cornflakes on the terrace from time to time, particularly in bad weather, for the birds, and within no time at all, they had been eaten. She decided to do the same. She sprinkled some cornflakes on the path leading from the shrubs to the pool house; her bait was set. Now all she had to do was to go back into the house and watch.

Standing back in her bedroom in the dark, Lucy stayed by the window and, within a short while, her idea worked. Ceefor left his hiding place to get the food, following it slowly to the pool house. Once inside, he decided to stay and take shelter from the rain.

For a long time, Lucy stayed at her bedroom window, watching the pool house door, watching the mesmerising rain as it bounced on the patio tiles outside. The sounds of her parents saying goodnight to their friends interrupted her thoughts and promptly she jumped into bed. But sleep is elusive when worrying thoughts keep popping up, and Lucy tossed and turned, frequently sneaking a look at the time. The rain throughout the night made a comforting sound on her window, but Lucy was eager for daybreak.

In the morning, before her parents got up, she crept outside, unlocking the kitchen door and anxiously made her way to the pool house. Ceefor had taken the milk and food, but he was not there. For a brief moment, she felt a tinge of concern, but when she bent down to feel the cushion, she realised it was still warm. Surely he couldn't be far, she said to herself.

And sure enough, she was right. From a distance, Ceefor peered through the shrubs. He had moved his position and was hiding near the palm tree, a little distance from the house. From his vantage point, he watched Lucy intently. She had always been kind to him, but he didn't understand how to trust her. The word trust was just a word to him. Unlike Ginge, who had learned from people's behaviour not to trust, Ceefor had never depended or relied on anyone until now. But this was something different. He had to stay close to Lucy; she was feeding him and he knew he had to build up his strength to get better.

Lucy knew Ceefor was watching her; she could feel his eyes on her back, following her every move. Rather than approach him again, she decided to go back into the house and watch him from her favourite spot at the window.

Ceefor sat alone, unapproachable, and as soon as the sun began to rise slowly over the Jalon Valley, the rains began to ease. Soon the sun would shine through the white clouds and within a short time everywhere would be dry again.

Ceefor moved quietly from behind the palm tree and back towards the pool house, hoping once more for food but then, as if he had changed his mind, he moved slowly onto the sunlit area in front of the pool. The sun was warm on the pool tiles and for a brief moment, Ceefor lay there, flat out in the sunshine, stretching his muscles and spreading his body, rolling over from side to side, enjoying the heat. He lay in that position with the sun warming him for a few minutes, before fleeing once more into the garden.

As usual, Lucy had breakfast that morning with her parents and, as they chatted, she knew that today being Tuesday, her mother would want her to go shopping at the local market. Every Tuesday, for as long as she could remember, the market was set up alongside the old stone church and surrounding area, around the fountain in the square. This was quite a mixed market, selling fresh vegetables, clothes and household goods, and it was also a meeting place. People from many of the local small villages around came to the village on Tuesdays and usually Lucy loved wandering about the old market place, enjoying a fresh orange drink in one of the many restaurants just off the square. But she also loved Ceefor and didn't want to leave him. She knew today would be difficult. Earlier that morning, she had filled the saucer in the pool house with more food and, although she didn't want to deliberately lie to her parents, she knew she couldn't tell them about Ceefor. But how could she get out of going to the market without them becoming suspicious?

As her mind mulled over this question, the phone rang in the lounge, breaking her concentration. She listened to her father talking and picked out some parts of the conversation that suddenly pleased her. The river was still high, and although the road was passable, the smaller bridge leading directly to the carpark was not, and so the market, she heard, was unlikely to be on. This delighted Lucy, but she didn't want to show it, so she said nothing.

Occasionally, when the weather changes from torrential rain to sunshine, there is sometimes the risk of thunderstorms. Some of these are spectacular, with sheet lightening that strikes across the sky, sending spidery flashes in all directions with loud bangs that vibrate across the valley. The sky can be seen with magenta hues of light and the sounds of thunder rolls around the valley until it eventually peters out into the distance. Sometimes Lucy got frightened when these storms erupted and many times her mum and dad would let her slip into their bed for the night.

Today, though, there was no storm and there was no market, and once Lucy was washed and dressed, she decided to continue to keep watch on Ceefor.

Over the next few days, as the weather continued to improve, Lucy tended her little friend. Each day she took food and water to him and every day, without exception, he raced off into the bushes whenever she approached too close, but he never went away. Instead, he chose to stay close to the house and, more importantly, near to Lucy.

Lucy adored Ceefor, but she also knew that now he was much better, she had to face the problem of what was going to happen to him when shortly she had to go back to England with her parents. She knew she didn't want to leave him. But strangely, Ceefor sensed something was about to happen too and he took the decision out of her hands. That evening, without warning, Ceefor left.

PART TWO
Spring

Spring arrived early the following year in Jalon. In the middle of February, the whole valley was bathed in almond blossom. Beautiful pink and white flowers smothered the trees throughout the valley and the wonderful scent lingered in the air. The temperatures had risen and soon the local farmers would be out on their small tractors, preparing the vineyards. The new crops of red and white grapes that made the Jalon wine would be picked and harvested in September/October. Up until now, the fields had lain dormant until the spring, and now the black stumps that formed rows of odd shaped vines had started to grow again.

This was a lovely time in the valley.

Ceefor had returned to the village at Christmas and had resumed his life of foraging for food and sleeping wherever there was shelter.

Lucy and her parents had left a few weeks after he disappeared but already she missed him. She had returned to England and from the moment she left she was counting the days to go back in the hope of seeing Ceefor.

Ginge had had a miserable time over the previous months of winter, but was still here, still hiding in the Nissen hut and still waiting for people to give her their leftover food.

A lot of kittens had been born in the rocks by the riverbed that spring. They had learned pretty quickly to stay near the bins at the bottom of the hill. This was where most of the houses up the mountainside put their rubbish, just before crossing the bridge to the village.

But there was fear amongst the older cats. Many of the younger cats had been disappearing overnight and Ceefor was not sure what was happening to them.

Unbeknown to Ceefor and the other cats, there had been an empty house halfway up the hill that had now had new people move in. The elderly couple didn't like cats, and as the cats kept straying into their garden at night, they had decided to take the matter into their own hands and get rid of them. This was frightening news and, but for Rock Rat, they would not have found this out.

Rock Rat wasn't really a rock rat as such, but the feral cats called him that. He was a fruit tree rat and lived on the fruits in the trees. The couple had devised a metal cage and left it in the garden with food inside, to encourage the cats to enter. Once inside the cage, the door flap closed, trapping them inside the cage. When a few cats were caught, the elderly couple would take the cats high up into the mountain and let them loose. These were the cat snatchers.

Although feral cats were a problem in Spain, many people living locally in the villages had formed a cat protection society to try to get the cats neutered so that they didn't have any more kittens, and tried to rescue them and get them good homes. But no one, it seemed, wanted an adult cat. Kittens were lovely and cuddly, and easier to get homes for, but feral cats were very difficult to catch or domesticate.

Ceefor had remained safe, but he was still cautious, despite now having known some kindness in his life. He had warmed to Lucy, but sadly to no one else.

Ceefor had run into the tramps of the road many times over the past few months. They were quite a team, Nero leading Blanco through the fields or through the village, always keeping their distance from people. Again, they had learned through people's behaviour who could be trusted and who could not. Even in the animal kingdom there was a moral code, a type of law that they understood. They learned quickly to be fearful, yet it took such a long time for them to learn to trust – such a little word with such responsibility.

One time in the village, Ceefor was minding his own business, sleeping on a wall near the village garage. He had got a good place high up over the garage in the sunshine and there he lay until dusk. As it cooled down, he watched as the restaurant waiters cleared away the tables and watched as Nero and Blanco nonchalantly ambled their way across the road to the restaurant where there was a garage directly opposite. The concrete forecourt was a good place to rest.

In the daytime, the heat had warmed the concrete ground but part of it was also under cover. During the day, this cover was shielded from the hot sun but, as evening descended, the concrete was still warm, so it was a good place to bed down for a cool night. Nero and Blanco used this spot a lot. It was in full view of the restaurant and if food was spilt onto the pavement, they could get it quickly. This particular restaurant always left a bowl of water outside for customers with dogs, so when no one was around they could get a fresh drink.

The night sky was lit this night with lots of stars and the air was still as Nero and Blanco settled down. In the distance, the sounds of dogs barking could be heard. Nero lifted his head slowly. He looked over at Blanco who had curled herself up for the night. The barking seemed to be getting louder and closer. Nero once more looked at Blanco. His ears pricked up and he eased himself up quietly, strutting to the middle of the street to see what was going on, and then disappearing around the corner.

Blanco was left on her own. She was thinner and weaker these days and still had sores on her legs. Her days as a tramp of the road were taking their toll on her. Quietly, she waited and waited, but there was no sign of Nero. After a while, seemingly alarmed by his disappearance, she got up slowly, easing her tired body off the ground. Then she barked just once. In the distance a single bark could be heard in the direction of Nero. She barked once more. Then from around the corner Nero appeared, heading straight towards Blanco. She eased herself down and curled up again. He settled down beside his loyal friend for the evening, with just the odd bark or two, more of a deterrent to anyone passing, or the watching rooftop cat. After that night, the tramps of the road were never seen again. No one knew what had happened to them or where they went. They simply disappeared as quickly as they had mysteriously arrived in the valley.

Ceefor continued to stay out of trouble for the majority of that summer and remained relatively well. The heat had meant that he stayed mostly under the cover of the undergrowth during the days and searched for food in the coolness of the evening. Sometimes he joined Ginge by the bins, but poor Ginge was struggling. The heat was too much for her and on many days she rarely left the Nissen hut. Usually, as soon as it because dusk, she came out and that was not always the time that people were around, so she had less and less to eat and, more importantly, nothing to drink. Occasionally some kind holidaymaker would bring food just for her and because they brought too much all in one go, she ate it so quickly that it made her sick. Once the holidaymakers left, Ginge was once again so hungry.

The Nissen hut had been a godsend for Ginge. It was a huge long hut that had been left there by the builders, storing all their equipment whilst they had built the houses on the hillside. When the work was finished, the Nissen hut was left locked and empty. Some time later, an eco-park was built alongside the Nissen hut, together with a new area for the bins. When Ginge had found this spot and, more particularly, the little hole to the side of it, she had been younger and had defended this small home of hers because of where it was situated. It was dry in the winter months and kept the sun off her in the summer. It was also close to the bins. But, with time, her age and ailing health were now her enemies and she had grown weak and vulnerable to illness.

Ceefor hadn't seen Ginge for ages, but this was nothing unusual. Some feral animals lived together in small groups, whilst others like Ceefor and Ginge seemed contented to live alone. Ceefor only made the journey up the mountain when it rained, except for one humid night to try to escape the onslaught of the fruit flies. He decided to try out his skills for hunting mice and headed up towards the Nissen hut. The undergrowth was thick with dried grass and weeds, and the trail upwards was far from easy. From sleeping and hunting in the campo, he had not been up this way for many days, so Ceefor took his time. The fruit flies seemed less annoying the higher up he walked, or maybe it was just a bit cooler and more bearable.

As Ceefor approached the hut, he slowed down momentarily in his tracks. Up ahead he could see a lifeless form lying by the roadside. He moved quietly and, as he got closer, he realised it was Ginge. Her strength had finally given up and she had simply got tired of life, laid down near some bushes and died. Her poor malnourished body, full of fleas, was still warm and she must have been making her way back to the Nissen hut, which was not too far from where she frequently prowled at night.

Somehow Ceefor could sense she had not long died, as he smelt her body and then for a short time he laid down next to her. Ginge had been frail and weak for some time, so maybe it was her time, but Ceefor was terribly saddened. He had known Ginge forever, and had had many wars with her since she had been a young cat. But they had, in their latter years, looked after each other's backs and all had the same fighting strength to stay alive in sometimes harsh conditions that kept them in the valley. Ceefor stayed with Ginge through that night and in the morning he returned to the campo. There he stayed for the next few days and when he returned to the mountainside, Ginge's body was gone.

Ceefor slept well that night, the first in a long time. As daylight beckoned, Ceefor had acquired a

new home, shelter from heat, protection from the wind and rain. He was now thinner, too, so he could squeeze into Ginge's place in the Nissen hut. It would be some time before he would come into contact with Lucy again, possibly when the rains started in late autumn.

Lucy though, constantly searched for Ceefor and many times their paths crossed momentarily, but Ceefor didn't see her. She still had her binoculars and still watched him from the back of her parents' car when they were out in the valley or within sight of the Nissen hut. The huge fondness for Ceefor that Lucy had when she first set eyes on him as a kitten never left her and each winter she hoped that the rains would come and block the bridge so Ceefor would return. But the rains didn't come that year and Ceefor never needed to take that long walk up the hillside. Not until another accident a couple of years later.

PART THREE
Two years later

It all began one morning, as Ceefor returned to the Nissen hut after a night of hunting in the orange groves. The weather was hot in August and fiestas were in full swing throughout the valley, especially in Jalon. Podenco, who shied away from people ever since she had been thrown out by her owners, had moved from the village up the mountain to escape the noise and crowds during the fiesta weeks.

Ceefor was unaware that Podenco had slept that night behind the Nissen hut but as he returned towards the path, it was soon obvious that Podenco had seen him. Ceefor was taken by surprise as Podenco barked and barked and chased him. Ceefor darted quickly up a nearby olive tree but, in the process, he manoeuvred himself awkwardly between two large, jagged stumps, one of which was a decaying hollow bark, and instantly Ceefor could feel himself slipping. His claws tried to grip the dry bark but it just wasn't holding his grip and turned to flakes of aged old bark as he slid. The rotted hole inside the bark wasn't big, but it was large enough to wedge a small, thin cat. Ceefor became trapped and try as he might, he couldn't free himself.

For several minutes, Podenco stood at the base of the tree, pondering what had just happened. One minute Ceefor was there and the next minute he had simply vanished. But Podenco wasn't fooled; she still had Ceefor's scent and she knew he was there somewhere, but where? For a few minutes more, she sat at the base of the olive tree, looking up into its branches in silence. But then the silence was broken by the sound of Ceefor meowing loudly, which in turn set Podenco off barking furiously once again.

People in cars going up and down the hillside stared and pointed in huge amusement at the sight of this dog barking relentlessly at a tree that, quite obviously to them, had nothing in it. But the incessant barking had intrigued one passing motorist and the couple decided to stop and investigate.

As the car reversed to the tree to see what the problem was, Podenco decided it was time to give up on this stupid idea and darted off down the road, leaving a wispy trail of dust in her wake.

Maybe lady luck was on Ceefor's side that day, or perhaps it was one of the many lives he challenged but, as the man and woman got out of the car, their young daughter stepped out too. It was Lucy, with her parents. From the car, Lucy has seen the white tip of a tail, but at first glance she didn't dare hope.

The muffled cries of Ceefor got louder, making Lucy's dad act quickly. He tried repeatedly to shake the tree, hoping to dislodge Ceefor, and when that didn't work, he collected a blanket from the car and simply grabbed hold of Ceefor's tail and pulled him out, wrapping him tightly in the blanket.

It was a tense moment. The blanket restrained him temporarily, but his natural feral instincts pushed him to squirm fiercely. As he started to fight to free himself, he saw her, from the corner of his eye, the young girl standing there, smiling. Lucy held her arms out and pleaded with her father to hand him to her. With the cat calming down somewhat, he reluctantly handed him to her whilst he got a box to put him in.

Her parents had agreed that they should take the cat home and help it get better, until they could sort out what to do next. Lucy sat next to the box in the back seat of the car and quietly murmured his name as they drove home. The sound of Lucy's voice and the gentleness of her tone quickly stirred up memories for Ceefor. It calmed him down momentarily until they reached the house, whereupon he quickly got agitated being in a box.

Lucy's father could see this, so he took Ceefor to the pool house and left the box open, adding a cautionary warning to Lucy not to go near him. But Lucy wondered how she could follow that advice, particularly when her parents insisted that because Ceefor was a wild cat, she could get hurt. Lucy knew Ceefor would not harm her or anyone else, but for the moment she heeded her father's advice and quietly stayed in the background.

For a number of days, she followed their caution but at night, when she looked out of her bedroom window, her gaze always focused on the pool house and then she allowed herself to look towards the night sky. In her mind, Lucy had made many wishes on those stars, and this night was no different. Firstly, she wished that she had told her parents the whole story about Ceefor in the beginning and had owned up to those silly little white lies she had told them. Guilt was sometimes a difficult thing to carry. She also wished that she had had someone to share her secret with, although she suspected that if she had told her parents the truth in the first place, she wouldn't now have a big secret. She also wished that she spent more time in Spain and yet, with that wish, she knew she would miss her friends. But mostly, as she stared into the clear black sky, she wished for Ceefor to get better.

With that, she rubbed her tired eyes and climbed into bed. She thought once more about her wishes and with that fell soundly asleep.

Over the next few days, there were moments that were harrowing. Ceefor, although not badly hurt, had sprained his previously injured leg and looked pitiful as he limped around the locked pool house. With obvious discomfort, he cried incessantly at times, which was alarming to hear, but whether it was because he was locked up or in pain was difficult to judge.

Lucy's parents slipped food and water into the pool house doorway every day, and in that respect they took charge of the situation in the ensuing days. Keeping him in the pool house with warmth, food and water paid off, and he rapidly made a recovery. Then, as he became more active and his limping decreased, they gradually started leaving the pool house door slightly open so that he could come and go as he pleased.

This was an important lesson for Lucy to learn: the freedom to choose. They explained that just because she had grown to love him didn't mean that Ceefor was hers to own. They also wanted her to remember that Ceefor was, and always would be, a feral cat. His instincts were intrinsic. Lucy didn't know what the word intrinsic meant, but she opened her dictionary and looked it up as her parents explained that his wild actions were needed for his survival.

Little by little, her parents worked on trying to obtain Ceefor's trust. They left the kitchen door open to see if Ceefor would venture in and, slowly, he did. But only on his terms. Ceefor would quietly creep in to the threshold of the doorway and occasionally he would sit there with his back to the outside world, just watching. Lucy would sit cross-legged on the floor opposite him, he looking in at her and she looking out at him.

Always that small personal space between them. Whenever she stretched out her hand to touch him, he recoiled. Any sudden movement or noise made him run for cover. But he was beginning to be less suspicious and would, at times, take food from her hand. He was also slowly putting on weight.

Lucy's parents watched and were enthralled with seeing this feral cat starting to respond. Lucy showed Ceefor her compassion and warmth and he responded to that. For the first time in his life, Ceefor had found someone who liked him enough to bring about that change, simply because she believed he deserved a chance. Her act of friendship was unconditional, wanting nothing in return. And her parents, in their many conversations about it, had to admit that Lucy, being an only child, might have benefited greatly from having a family pet.

They discussed this and realised that sometimes grown-ups don't know everything, they don't have all the answers. People can only make decisions that seem right at the time, even if it turns out to be a wrong decision later. But they also agreed that no decision is ever a bad decision, as long as you learn something from it.

Lucy was growing up with caring, altruistic values which they were so proud of and she had shown that in the love and respect she had for Ceefor.

But now this problem with Ceefor was not getting resolved and was fast becoming everyone's dilemma, one they had not come across before, so had little experience to fall back on.

Lucy's parents talked this over for hours, but there just didn't seem to be an answer. Perhaps, when you can't see the wood for the trees, the answer is there in front of you all along but you just can't see it. Sometimes, too, a decision can be taken quite literally out of your hands.

The next day, shortly after Ceefor had been fed, he meandered off and never came back. A thorough search of the pool area and the mountainside behind the house failed to show any sighting of Ceefor. And as darkness fell, no amount of calling his name would bring him out of the shadows, back to the house. Even tapping his plate with food didn't entice him back.

At first, Lucy was upset, sad in a way that Ceefor had perhaps once again decided he wanted to go and leave her. But then, not seeing him in his favourite spots in the village, she became anxious that something awful had happened to him. Fraught with concerns for his safety and weary from crying, Lucy was pleased that this time that she had someone else to share her worries with – her parents. She didn't need to keep her concerns and fears to herself or hide them. This was such a relief. The power of sharing meant that she was not alone.

The days ahead were long and tiring, whilst Lucy continued to be vigilant and kept searching and wondering what could have happened to Ceefor, with posters pinned to every doorway. But Ceefor was not to be found.

Soon it would be time for Lucy and her parents

to leave Spain once more, and this brought fresh concerns for Ceefor's safety. Lucy's new centre of focus in her questions to her mum were what would happen to Ceefor when they returned to England? How would she know if he was all right and was found?

Her parents understood this anxiety, but even they couldn't answer those questions. All they could do was try to quell her fears by giving her their own reassuring advice. They knew that the good thing about advice, in whatever form it's given, is that it can be adapted. It can be changed to whatever you think is the right thing to do or just store it, so that when it's time to make decisions, there are options.

Lucy trusted her parents implicitly and took their advice in, that when Ceefor was hungry he would return. And that is exactly what happened two days later. Shortly after sunrise, Ceefor quietly returned. He had been missing for eight days, eight very long days in Lucy's eyes.

His forlorn figure could be seen from the kitchen window as he hovered outside the closed pool house. Lucy was in bed and heard the commotion in the kitchen with excited voices. Then her mum shouted to her the long-awaited news. Ceefor was back.

Lucy shot out of bed, delighted. Thanking her lucky stars, she thought maybe dreams do come true if you wish hard enough, as she raced outside in her bare feet to see him.

Ceefor was thinner but, just as Lucy's mum had

predicted, he was hungry and headed straight to the pool house for food. Ceefor had always known where to go for food. When the heavy rains came and the bridge was blocked, he always made the journey up the hill to Lucy's house, so many times. But through the kindness of Lucy and her parents, he now made the choice to return even when there was no rain. Lucy felt privileged to realise that. She understood it was on his terms. So however long he chose to stay now was really up to him.

Ceefor was, and always would be, a feral cat. He was able to recognise who to trust and these instincts had helped him survive. He knew what pain was and he knew fear. He had laid down next to Ginge when she had died, so he almost certainly felt grief. But he also knew what freedom was. So maybe the answer to Lucy's question about Ceefor, when she asked her mum what was going to happen to Ceefor, was simply to see what Ceefor would decide for himself. He had found friendship in Lucy, and maybe something else as well.

Lucy knew she would always love Ceefor. She had loved him right from the first moment she set eyes on him as a little kitten. But she also knew that Ceefor would not be tamed and he wasn't hers to keep. He would always be in charge of his own destiny, his own fate. Because Ceefor was born to be free and I suppose who are we to argue with that.